The Crazy Collector

by

Diana Hendry

Illustrated by Kirstin Holbrow

You do not need to read this page -
just get on with the book!

First published in Great Britain by Barrington Stoke Ltd
10 Belford Terrace, Edinburgh EH4 3DQ
Copyright © 2001 Diana Hendry
Illustrations © Kirstin Holbrow
The moral right of the author has been asserted in
accordance with the Copyright, Designs and
Patents Act 1988
ISBN 1-902260-83-X
Printed by Polestar AUP Aberdeen Ltd

MEET THE AUTHOR - DIANA HENDRY

What is your favourite animal?
Dog
What is your favourite boy's name?
Hamish, my son's name
What is your favourite girl's name?
Kate, my daughter's name
What is your favourite food?
Chips!
What is your favourite music?
Mozart
What is your favourite hobby?
Playing the piano

MEET THE ILLUSTRATOR - KIRSTIN HOLBROW

What is your favourite animal?
My dog, Pewter Plum
What is your favourite boy's name?
Flash
What is your favourite girl's name?
Vanilla
What is your favourite food?
Sprouts
What is your favourite music?
Pop
What is your favourite hobby?
Rowing on the River Wye
and walking my dog

For Dorothy Grandma -
with love

Contents

Chapter 1
A Plug In Her Pocket

I don't know where my sister Tess got the idea. Mum says she's a magpie, always collecting things. I think she's got Collector Mania. I think she was born with it.

It began with dummies. Yes, dummies! When she was a baby she had about a dozen of them hanging from her cot and

pram. By the time she was four it was plugs. That was a really embarrassing one. You'd think plugs would be hard to collect. I mean we only have three in our house – the sink plug in the kitchen, the bath plug and the washbasin plug. That meant that Tess had to collect other people's plugs. Well, I'm being kind. She had to steal other people's plugs. Wherever we went, Tess would come home with a plug in her pocket.

Of course nobody called it stealing because Tess was only four. Four and strong enough to yank a plug off its chain. And she looked very sweet, my sister, with her hair in little ginger bunches and her nose all freckles. People thought it rather funny when she went off with their plug. At least they *said* they did. I don't suppose it really *is* funny if you're just about to have a bath and suddenly discover you don't have a plug.

Mum kept saying Tess was too little to know any better. But there was a really good reason why Tess liked plugs. She liked the way the water went whirling down the plug hole when you pulled the plug out. She could play with a plug for hours, shouting, "Whirly, Whirly, Whirly! Twirly, Twirly, Twirly!"

There was no good reason for the next craze – the collection of boxes that began to grow under her bed. Matchboxes. Shoe boxes. Cardboard boxes that someone had packed a present in at Christmas. Big supermarket boxes. Those boxes you get from the corner shop with Cox's Apple Pippin on the side and bumpy, purple paper at the bottom where the apples sit. Old, wooden boxes Tess bought from junk shops with her pocket money. Boxes covered with shells. Tin boxes with pictures on the lids. Tiny, velvet-lined boxes that had once held gold rings. Money boxes without any money in them. Oh, and egg boxes. Loads and loads of egg boxes.

In fact none of Tess's boxes had anything inside them.

"Tess," I said to her when she was six, "a box is for keeping things in."

"I know, James," Tess told me, with one of her scornful, I-am-not-an-idiot looks. "But I like to think about what I *might* put in them."

"I suppose you'll use them for whatever stupid thing you decide to collect next," I said and I gave her look for look.

I wish I'd never said that. I saw her eyes suddenly brighten. I thought I'd better warn Mum. "She's thinking about what to collect next," I said.

Mum groaned. "Let's hope it's small," she said. "Do you think she might choose buttons or bottle-tops this time?"

But buttons didn't appeal to Tess, nor did bottle-tops. Stones did.

It's amazing how many different kinds of stones there are really. And all sizes. Tess used to stagger home from school with a bag full of them. They weighed down the pockets of her jacket.

I quite liked the stones. Some of them had nice shapes. They were smooth or rough. You could nurse a smooth, round one in your pocket and that was rather nice.

They were all shades of grey, brown and black. Some of them had flecks of different colours. Some were like little chunks of marble. We broke one stone open and it had a milky middle.

Tess spent hours laying the stones out on her bedroom floor and then packing them into her boxes. She stuck labels on the boxes. Mum had to write them for her but Tess knew what they all were.

"Slate isn't really a stone," I said to Tess.

"That's what you think," said Tess. "My teacher says it comes from rocks – from cliffs. There's quarries full of slate. So there!"

Actually I really liked the slate. It was so thin and fine and you could write on it in chalk. Mum said that once upon a time children used slates and chalk in school, instead of paper and pencils. I got Tess to give me a piece of slate as a swap for – you've guessed it – another box.

Anyway, it got to the point when Mum and I began to think that all those stones would fall through the floor of Tess's bedroom and into the living room below. We might even be killed one day by an avalanche of stones.

"ENOUGH IS ENOUGH!" Mum said very loudly and slowly, so we knew she meant it. "You can choose your favourites and keep them in ONE box," Mum said. "The rest will have to go. And the boxes."

I expected Tess to make an awful fuss. But she didn't. She was bored with boxes and stones. She'd got a new craze.

It wasn't long before Mum and I began to wish she'd stuck with the stones. Stamp collecting only lasted three weeks but we wished it had lasted longer. Or that someone could have talked her into collecting marbles or Pokémon cards. Anything! Anything!

Because what Tess decided to collect next was ... a family!

Chapter 2
A Gaggle of Grans

I had better explain. Of course we are a family, Mum, Tess and I. The Morris family. One of those small families who don't have all those extras other people seem to have – aunts and uncles, first cousins and second cousins and third and fourth and fifth ones. We do have a Dad, only he lives in America and one day we're going to visit him, Tess and I.

You could say we're a kind of global family. Dad's parents – our Grandad and Grandma – live with him in America. Mum's Dad is dead and Mum's Mum lives in Australia. We call her our Down-Under Gran.

Of course we get presents from them on birthdays and at Christmas time and sometimes there are telephone calls. If we had a computer I could send them e-mails. But we haven't. Mum's saving up for one. Mum also says that one day, if we win the lottery, we'll go on a round-the-world trip and visit American Grandma and Grandad and Down-Under Gran. But I can't see us winning the lottery. Mum often forgets to do it. Mum and Dad had no brothers and sisters which explains why we don't have aunts and uncles.

When I hear other kids talking about their grandparents I tell them that I've got a Grandma in America and a Grandma in Australia and they're dead jealous and ask when I'm going to visit them. And I say, "Maybe this summer. Maybe next ..." That 'maybe' makes me feel I'm not exactly telling a lie.

Deep inside I do sometimes think it would be nice just to have a Gran who lived down the road. A Gran you could just call in and see whenever you felt like it. A Gran who might help you out when you were a bit low on pocket money.

Maybe Tess felt the same way. I think her mad idea of collecting a family began that term when she moved into a new class. Everyone in Tess's class had at least one Gran. One girl, Mandy Edwards, had three because her Mum had married again, so she got an extra one.

The boys in Tess's class were always being taken to football matches by their

Grandads. The girls got taken shopping or to the cinema by their Grans.

"If I had a Gran," Tess said to Mum, "a nearby sort of Gran, I bet she'd buy me those new jeans and I bet she'd baby-sit when you were at evening class. I bet she'd invite me to stay the night and I bet she'd *always* be on my side."

Tess is very good at making Mum feel guilty for things that aren't Mum's fault at all.

So I said to Tess, "I bet she'd make you tidy your bedroom and comb your hair and clean the bath – if she had any sense, she'd be on *my* side."

"There's no point in talking about it," said Mum in a worn-out sort of voice. "I can't just invent a Gran."

That made Tess think. She went off to bed muttering, "Invent a Gran. Invent a Gran. Invent a Gran. Invent a Gran." By morning, she'd done three posters.

The words were bad enough. I mean if people from school saw the posters we'd never hear the end of it. I could just imagine Roy Mason, that loudmouth, saying, 'Oh, so you want a cuddly Gran do you? A nice cuddly-wuddly Gran!'

But there wasn't just writing on the posters. Tess had done something far worse. She'd stuck on some photos. And they weren't photos of how we look now. Oh no. Tess had stuck on BABY photos. She'd sneaked them out of Mum's photo album. There was one of me in my baby bath, for goodness sake! And there was Tess looking ever so cute in a frilly bonnet and sitting up in her pram.

I saw the posters in Tess's bedroom. Mum had sent me up there to tell her to get a move on or we'd be late for school. Tess was just adding a few flowers to the last poster and surrounding the photos with kisses.

"What are you going to do with those?" I yelled at her.

"Sssh!" hissed Tess. "Don't tell Mum. I'm going to put one in the newsagent's window and one on the lamp-post and ..."

"The lamp-post ...?" I groaned. "People put posters about lost kittens on lamp-posts."

"Well, this one is about a lost Gran," said Tess.

"They're not lost," I said angrily. "One's in America and one's in Australia."

"OK, OK!" said Tess. "Maybe not lost, but far away. It's the same thing."

I could tell Tess was getting angry now. By the look of those posters, she'd been up half the night doing them.

"Where's the third poster going?" I asked.

"There's a billboard near the bus stop," said Tess.

"That's where they advertise pop concerts and clubs and the latest fizzy drink," I told her. "They don't advertise for Grans."

"They just lack imagination," said Tess. She was in one of her stroppy moods now. She may be my little sister but she's got a very big temper. When she's in a stroppy mood her eyes flash and she tosses her hair about. She did that now.

"But why baby photos?" I pleaded.

"Because, idiot, all Grans like babies," Tess snapped.

"But we're not babies," I said, feeling

just like the idiot Tess had called me. "I mean I'm eleven, you're nine – we're a long way off being babies."

"When they meet us, they'll love us," said Tess. "That's what Grans are like."

"They?" I said. "They? How many Grans are you planning to adopt?"

"That depends," said Tess, "on how many apply," and she slipped the posters in her school bag and stomped down the stairs.

"If Mum finds out she'll go ballistic!" I whispered.

Tess turned on me. "Look," she said, "do you or don't you want a Gran?"

I couldn't say a word because the truth is I *did* want a Gran. In fact I wouldn't mind a Gran and a Grandad. I didn't tell Tess that. But I didn't need to. She knew what I was thinking from the look on my face.

"Well then," she whispered back, "you won't say a word to Mum, will you?"

"But she's going to find out!" I squeaked. "When our Gran arrives."

"Our Gran! Our Gran!" mimicked Tess with a grin. "Look, if I ask Mum if I can advertise for a Gran she'll say no. But if a Gran just turns up – well, she'll love Mum like she'll love us. And Mum will love her back. Mum just doesn't realise she needs a Gran."

I didn't feel so sure.

Chapter 3
Stars

You wouldn't believe just how many wannabe Grans there are in the world. Well, never mind the world, just in Lorton.

Tess put the posters up on our way to school. She put one outside the newsagent, one on a lamp-post and one on the billboard by the bus stop. This meant we were late and got a ticking-off from Mrs Wiggins, the teacher on duty.

When we got home from school Mum was in the living room giving tea to eight wannabe Grans. There were three squashed up on the sofa. Another two were sitting on kitchen chairs. One was on the rocking chair from Mum's bedroom. A very cuddly Gran was sitting crosslegged on my bean bag and the eighth was twirling round and round on the piano stool.

There was a chorus of "Aaaaaahs!" as we came into the room and a sort of Chinese whisper went round from Gran to Gran to Gran, "Here they are! Here they are! Here they are!" as if we were pop stars. I suppose that's what grandchildren really are to their grandparents. Stars. Very Important People.

Actually one of the Grans didn't think so. She got up from her kitchen chair, looked us up and down and said, "These two won't do, I wanted babies!" And out she marched.

The Gran on the piano stool did a few more twirls and laughed.

"Tess, dear," said Mum in that very sugary voice she only uses when she's very, very mad, "these ladies all want to be your Gran. Isn't that the strangest thing?"

I didn't know then how Mum knew it was Tess, and not me, who'd put up the posters. We learnt, later, that she'd gone down to have a look at the poster wrapped round the lamp-post. She saw it was Tess's writing of course.

Tess went bright red and hung her head.

There's something you should know about my little sister. I hate to say it, but she looks very, very cute with those ginger bunches and freckles. Right now she looked as if butter wouldn't melt in her mouth.

"Poor little thing!" said Rocking Chair Gran. "Don't be cross with her, Mrs Morris, I thought it was such a sweet thing to do."

And the six other Grans all nodded their heads in agreement.

"Sweet!" echoed Mum. "This poor little thing, as you call her, could drive anyone round the wall in five minutes flat!"

"I can see she really needs a Gran," said Sofa Gran One as if she thought Mum was an awful Mum.

"And so does the lad," said the Gran on my bean bag. I was glad they were thinking about me too. And I liked the look of Bean Bag Gran. She had a nice smile and she looked both cuddly and strong – as if she

SOFA GRAN 1

SOFA GRAN 2

SOFA GRAN 3

KITCHEN CHAIR GRAN 1

BEAN BAG GRAN

ROCKING CHAIR GRAN

KITCHEN CHAIR GRAN 2

PIANO STOOL GRAN

could kick a football as well as giving you a good hug when you needed one.

"And maybe," said Bean Bag Gran, "it would be nice for you, Mrs Morris, to have a Gran around. Someone helping out now and again. Giving you a hand. Perhaps cooking tea some nights. Or baby-sitting. I mean children-sitting," she added quickly.

I could see Mum melting a little just at the thought of not having to cook the tea.

"I'd like you to know that I'm very good at knitting," said Sofa Gran Two.

"I can play the piano," offered Piano Stool Gran. "I could give them both lessons."

And then they were all at it. Telling us what they were good at. Trying to go one better. It was like some kind of awful job interview only no-one was doing the interviewing. There was very little those seven Grans couldn't do. They could cook, they could knit, they could swim, they could sing. One knew everything there was to know about birds. One did judo. One used to teach maths. One was a gardener. Bean Bag Gran said she'd been a racing car driver. I liked the sound of that.

"Hold it! Hold it!" cried Mum. "You all sound absolutely brilliant. But *nobody* has seven Grans!"

"Tess and James should choose," said Piano Gran.

"I don't want to choose," I said at once. I could see that all those Grans were longing to have us as their grandchildren. I knew the ones we didn't choose would be really miserable. I wanted Bean Bag Gran. I badly wanted Bean Bag Gran. But I wasn't going to say so.

"I don't want to choose either," said Tess, "because you're all so lovely."

There was another long "Aaaaaaah" from the starstruck Grans.

"Creep!" I muttered to Tess.

"Let's have a lottery," said Sofa Gran One.

"Good idea!" said Sofa Gran Two. (She was the one who did judo.)

Mum fetched some paper and we cut it up into seven pieces and wrote GRAN just on one. Tess wrote:

on the other six pieces. Then we folded them up. Mum found an old hat and we put the seven pieces of paper inside and jiggled them about.

The Grans each had to take a piece of paper.

It was an awful moment. The three Sofa Grans looked really tense.

"My only daughter died," said one of them, "and she didn't have any children. I've wanted a grandchild for years."

"My son and his family are in Hong Kong," said Piano Gran. "I've never met my youngest grandchild. A little boy. Name of Ben."

Mum began to look quite tearful and I could see Tess was about to cry too.

"Well," said Bean Bag Gran, "may the best Gran win!" And she put her hand in the hat and pulled out a piece of paper.

Chapter 4
The Granny Can-Can

Piano Gran won. Piano Gran hitched up her skirts and danced round the room. Then she gave first me and then Tess an enormous hug. "Say it!" said Piano Gran. "Just let me hear you say it! I want to hear you call me Granny."

"Granny," said Tess. Even though her voice was muffled – coming as it did from inside the hug – I knew Tess was thinking what I was thinking. That it was a shame about all those other Grans.

I'd taken a quick look at Bean Bag Gran. She pulled a face at me and held up her piece of paper that said:

Don't get me wrong. I liked Piano Gran. I thought she'd be a lot of fun. Also our piano has sat there for ages with no-one able to play it. But Piano Gran was over-the-top jolly. All that twirling about on the piano stool had almost made me dizzy. I thought she might not be the sort of Gran you'd want if you were feeling rotten and just wanted to be with someone quiet and comforting.

The other Grans were all looking really upset. The Sofa Grans were crying. Kitchen Chair Gran stood up looking very huffy and said, "Well, I know when I'm not wanted. I'm sure there are lots of other children out there wanting a Gran. Nicer children."

Then Tess had her second bright idea. "Wait!" she cried. "We've got seven wannabe Grans here ..."

"So?" said Kitchen Chair Gran, who was halfway to the door.

"I've got it!" said Bean Bag. "Seven days of the week. Seven Grans!"

"That's it!" said Tess.

The Grans all cheered. Piano Gran did another twirl on the piano stool and began playing a really jazzy tune. Bean Bag started dancing and soon we were all joining in.

"It's the Granny Can-Can!" cried Piano Gran.

But if you ask me, all the Grans were doing a different dance. Bean Bag's dance looked more like a Highland Fling. The Sofa Grans were jiving. Kitchen Chair Gran and Rocking Chair Gran were singing 'Hands, Knees and Boomps-a-Daisy!' even though it didn't go with the music at all. Whenever they got to the Boomps-a-Daisy bit, they bumped their bums together and laughed their heads off.

One thing Tess and I learnt about Grans that day is that they run out of puff rather quickly. Very soon they'd all collapsed on the floor and Mum had to make more tea. Then they all began talking at once about who was going to be Monday Gran and who would be Tuesday Gran and who would do what and when.

"James and Tess could come and have tea at my house on a Wednesday," said Sofa Gran One.

"I'd like to take them shopping on Saturday afternoon," said Sofa Gran Two.

In no time at all it was going to be piano lessons on Monday, judo on Tuesday, tea on Wednesday, a film on Thursday, extra maths (uggh) on Friday, shopping on Saturday and bird watching on Sunday.

"Hold on!" said Mum. "When am I going to see them?"

Then they started all over again. Mum had to send out for pizza because they kept getting the days of the week in a muddle. By the time they got round to asking us what *we* wanted, Tess had fallen asleep on the rug and I was wondering if I was going to have any time to myself ever again. I went up to bed and left them to sort things out. I poked my nose into Tess's room on my way. There, on the floor, was a list called 'Collecting a Family'.

I was a bit miffed that Tess wanted another brother. Wasn't I good enough? And there wasn't a Grandad on the list.

Uncles...
Aunts...
Cousins...
Second cousins
Brothers...
Sisters...

Chapter 5

First Cousins, Second Cousins and Brothers Unlimited

"I've sorted them out," Mum said the next morning, "your seven Grans."

"I wouldn't mind," I said, "if Tess had six Grans and I had one."

"You want Bean Bag, I suppose," said Tess. "Talk about having favourites.

Anyway we're getting a different Gran every day."

"It isn't going to work that way," said Mum. "If we had a different Gran every day, we'd be quite worn out. We decided on a Gran a week. So it would be Sofa Gran One in the first week and Sofa Gran Two in the second week and so on."

"What? Every single day?" I asked.

"You're so ungrateful," said Tess. "I can't wait to tell them at school that I've got seven Grans. They'll be green with envy!"

"No, not every single day," Mum said and she ruffled my hair like she does sometimes when she knows how I'm feeling. "Maybe just once or twice during the week. Apart from Piano Gran that is. You're both to have piano lessons every Thursday afternoon."

"Great!" I said.

"I wish we'd found a Guitar Gran," said Tess.

"Now who's being ungrateful?" I said.

In fact, it all worked out really well. Life with seven Grans was quite different from life without them. It was better. It was much more fun.

Bean Bag and I went fishing. Bean Bag had an old car. An 'old banger' Mum called it and she told Bean Bag that she was on no account to show me how to be a racing car driver. I was to watch the speedometer and make sure Bean Bag never drove over 50 miles per hour.

The Sofa Grans One and Two had become very friendly, so they decided to share their week. They took Tess to the Museum and Tess loved it:

a) because there were lots of collections of things and

b) because they always had doughnuts in the café afterwards.

Kitchen Chair Gran gave us all Sunday lunch and it was utterly yummy. So we didn't mind too much when she gave us an extra maths lesson on Fridays.

Rocking Chair Gran taught us judo. I'm hoping I'll be a black belt one of these days. And Tess and I can now play duets, thanks to Piano Gran.

Sofa Gran Three took us to watch birds down by the river. We saw huge herons and things and got really wet and muddy. On the way back, we saw two magpies. "One

for sorrow, two for joy," said Sofa Gran
Three.

Mum really enjoyed the Grans too. She
was doing an evening course on computers
and she didn't have to worry about finding
anyone to look after us when she was out.
And she had lots more time to do the things
she liked doing – reading and gardening.
Often one or other of the Grans came round
while we were at school, just to have a chat
with Mum.

Mum said she really liked that. She said
she hadn't realised how much she missed
her own Mum.

Tess told everyone at school about her
seven Grans. She brought her best friend
Liz Tully home to meet the Sofa Grans and
the Kitchen Chair Gran. She wrote an essay
about the Grans for her school project and
got an 'A' for it. And she went about the

house looking really smug. She had about five thousand new scrunchies for her ginger bunches – presents from the Grans of course – and she was forever preening herself in the mirror.

I grabbed that 'Collecting a Family' list from beside her bed one Saturday morning and waved it under her nose.

"What's all this about then?" I asked. "I suppose seven Grans aren't enough for you. You want seven aunts and seven uncles and a few dozen cousins. You've got Collector Mania. And you want another brother as well."

I was really surprised by what Tess did next. She burst into tears and gave me a huge hug.

"You're the bestest brother ever," she said. "I didn't think we were going to have seven Grans. That list was a just-in-case list. In case we didn't get a Gran at all."

I hugged her back. "I'm glad you did it," I said. "I'm glad you wrote those 'Wanted' posters and I'm glad we've got seven Grans."

Tess wiped her eyes and grinned at me. "But a few cousins would be nice too, don't you think?"

"Enough is enough!" I said, in a voice just like Mum's.

So everything seemed to be going really well. The Morris family had grown. We'd become a big family and whenever we could, we all talked about 'Our Grans'.

That was before the party. Before The Very Embarrassing Moment.

Chapter 6
Bellies and Belly Buttons

Mum's birthday and my birthday are just two days apart in August. Mum was going to be forty.

"Grey hairs soon," said Mum, "I'm not sure I like the idea of that."

"Nonsense," said Bean Bag Gran. "Forty is ..."

"Please do not tell me that life begins at forty," said Mum. "All the Grans have told me that already."

"I wasn't going to," said Bean Bag. "I was just going to say that out of beginnings, middles and ends, I think middles are the best."

"Hmmph!" said Mum.

The party was Bean Bag's idea. On my birthday I was to have my own treat. I was going to a film with four of my mates, followed by fish and chips and a sleepover at my house.

"We could have a surprise party for your Mum," said Bean Bag. "All the Grans, your Mum, you and Tess."

She'd no sooner thought of a surprise party than all the Grans got busy planning it. They made a cake – with candles of course. Piano Gran made them all practise a singsong of Mum's favourite tunes. Sofa Gran Two amazed us all by saying she could do a belly dance and asked us if she could do it at the party.

"You bet!" said Tess. "And you can teach the rest of us."

"I don't think I want to do a belly dance," I said.

Bean Bag Gran just laughed, "Don't worry love," she said, "we'll need an audience. That can be you."

Tess and I had a really hard time keeping the party a secret from Mum. In the morning we gave her our birthday cards.

"I'll give you your present tonight," Tess told Mum.

"Me too," I said.

Mum tried not to look disappointed. It was a dull start to a birthday. Then after school it was difficult to get her to dress up in her velvet trousers and sequin top.

"It's your birthday," said Tess. "You've got to dress up a bit."

"Well, I thought we'd just have supper on trays in front of the telly," said Mum. "There's no point in dressing up for that."

"Yes there is," said Tess. "Please, Mum. *We're* going to wear something special." So Mum went upstairs to change and five minutes later all the Grans arrived. All the Grans except Bean Bag.

The Grans burst into *Happy Birthday to You* as Mum came down the stairs. In next to no time the table was laid with sausages

on sticks, sandwiches, home-made biscuits, apple pie and strawberries and cream. Right in the middle was Mum's birthday cake. Mum was thrilled to bits. And still Bean Bag hadn't arrived.

"Where can she have got to?" I asked Tess. "After all, this party was her idea."

"Maybe that old banger of hers has broken down," Tess said.

That just made me feel more worried than ever. Bean Bag knew everything there was to know about car engines. She could fix anything. But she did drive very fast and if she thought she was going to be late ...

The other Grans didn't seem at all worried about the missing Bean Bag.

"Don't you worry, dear," said Sofa Gran One. "She'll be here. I think she may have a special surprise for you."

I almost forgot to worry about Bean Bag when I watched Mum, Tess and the Grans all doing the belly dance. You wouldn't think there were so many different sorts of bellies and belly buttons. I laughed till I cried.

They were all in the middle of the belly dance when the doorbell rang.

"Bean Bag Gran!" I said and ran to open the door.

But there on the doorstep was a chubby, little woman with a smile as big as her suitcase. I knew that smile from somewhere and yet I felt sure I'd never seen her before in my life.

"You've got to be James!" said this stranger and she dropped her suitcase and threw her arms round me.

"What ...? Who ...?" I started to say, when I heard Tess and Mum behind me.

"Mum!" cried Mum.

"You're Down-Under Gran!" cried Tess.

And that's who it was.

"Thought I'd surprise you on your birthday!" said Down-Under Gran and she gave Mum a big hug. "I can see you're having a party already," said Down-Under Gran walking into the living room.

All the Grans stopped dancing and hid their bellies.

"Well, chucks, introduce me to your friends," said Down-Under Gran to Tess and me.

And that was the really embarrassing moment.

How was Down-Under Gran going to feel about all these other Grans?

"Well," Tess began, "this is Sofa Gran One and this is Piano Gran and this is ..."

But she stopped when the doorbell rang again. And this time it was Bean Bag. And Bean Bag was with a big, tall man in a naval officer's uniform.

Bean Bag was grinning all over her face.

"This is my husband, Jim," she said. "He's been away at sea. I've just picked him up from his ship. He's on leave."

Jim held out his hand to me. "You must be James," he said. "I've been feeling kind of left out of things. Do you think you've got room for a Grandad in your collection of Grans?"

"You bet!" I said. "Only things are a little tricky at the moment."

I took them both – Bean Bag Gran and Bean Bag Grandad – into the living room.

Somehow I expected Down-Under Gran to be really mad at us for replacing her with seven other Grans.

But she wasn't a bit mad. Tess was sitting on her knee and telling her just how much she'd missed having a Gran and all about the posters and the Grans arriving and then the lottery and how we'd decided that each Gran should have her own week.

And our Down-Under Gran just couldn't stop laughing.

At last, when she'd wiped her eyes and Mum had cut her a piece of birthday cake,

Down-Under Gran said, "And what were you all doing when I arrived?"

So Sofa Gran Two explained about the belly dancing and Down-Under Gran said that was something she'd always wanted to try. So they all began again.

Only this time there were two of us in the audience. Me and Grandad Bean Bag.

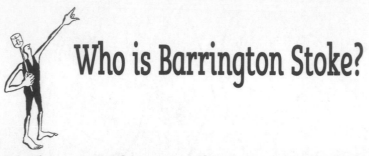

Who is Barrington Stoke?

Barrington Stoke was a famous and much-loved story-teller. He travelled from village to village carrying a lantern to light his way. He arrived as it grew dark and when the young boys and girls of the village saw the glow of his lantern, they hurried to the central meeting place. They were full of excitement and expectation, for his stories were always wonderful.

Then Barrington Stoke set down his lantern. In the flickering light the listeners were enthralled by his tales of adventure, horror and mystery. He knew exactly what they liked best and he loved telling a good story. And another. And then another. When the lantern burned low and dawn was nearly breaking, he slipped away. He was gone by morning, only to appear the next day in some other village to tell the next story.

Barrington Stoke would like to thank all its readers for commenting on the manuscript before publication and in particular:

Nicola Bissett
Simon Dodd
Paul Dawber
Katy Graham
Nikki Griffith
Jan Harrison
Douglas Hoggan
Alan Jackson
Martin Keeping
Holly Kennedy
Freddy Loudon

Adeel Mahmood
Camilla Morris
Philippa Morris
Samantha Newman
Lauren Pendleton
Cameron Ross
Andrew Scott
Leah Simnor
Charlie Suen
Catherine Waite
Kelsey Wilson

Become a Consultant!

Would you like to give us feedback on our titles before they are published? Contact us at the address or website below - we'd love to hear from you!

Barrington Stoke, 10 Belford Terrace, Edinburgh EH4 3DQ
Tel: 0131 315 4933 Fax: 0131 315 4934
E-mail: info@barringtonstoke.demon.co.uk
Website: www.barringtonstoke.co.uk

If you loved this story, why don't you read . . .

Pompom

by Michaela Morgan

Have you ever wished you had a dog? Paul dreams of having a champion dog to improve his image. It will give him something to boast about and help him with the bullies. But things go badly wrong – or do they? Discover how Paul finds out that looks are not everything.

Visit our website!
www.barrringtonstoke.co.uk